# DUG IN DANGER

Written and Illustrated by Shoo Rayner

W
FRANKLIN WATTS
LONDON•SYDNEY

# Dug's Bronze Age Family

Dug       Woof

Over 3,000 years ago, Dug's family found tin in riverbeds. They lived by a river in the far southwest of Britain. Join Dug in his perilous mission to find the largest tinstone in the roaring, raging river.

Mini       Dad

# Chapter One

"There's a prize for whoever finds the largest tinstone!" declared Dad.

"Me!" said Mini. "I'll find the biggest!"

"Bet I find a bigger one!" Dug ran towards the river. Woof barked and chased after him. "Ruff, ruff!"

"Stop!" shouted Dad. "The river is deep and flowing fast. You'll drown if you fall in!"
Dug and Woof skidded to a halt.
"Sorry, Dad!" said Dug. Then Dad pulled a shiny, metal disc from his bag.

4

"First we must give our gift to the river. We must keep the river happy or it will get angry," he explained.

"Can I throw it in, Dad?" asked Dug.

"Okay," said Dad. "When I nod, throw it into the deepest part of the river."

Dug hugged the bright, metal disc to his chest. Woof couldn't take her eyes off it.

"Oh, River!" Dad chanted, "Here is our gift.
Please bring us good weather and good luck
so we can find the biggest tinstones!"
Then he nodded at Dug.

Dug threw the disc into the sky. It flashed
as it spun through the air.

# Chapter Two

Woof ran after it. The disc fell and
splashed into the water. Woof leapt
into the wild, raging river.

"Woof! Come back!" Dug yelled.

Woof's head popped up above the water. She gripped the shiny disc firmly in her teeth. She had saved the shiny disc for Dug!

The wild water swept Woof away down
the raging river.

"Woof!" yelled Dug.

"Howl!" said Woof, holding on to the disc.

Dug raced along the riverbank.

"Woof! Keep your head up! I'll save you!"

Dug found a long stick and reached across the wild water.

"Hold on to this!" he yelled.

Woof let go of the disc. It sank into the murky water. Woof grabbed the stick with her teeth and Dug pulled her out of the river. Woof shook the water off her fur.

"Ahhh! That's freezing!" yelled Dug.

Mini looked scared. Her eyes were wide.
"The river will be angry with us now!" she
wailed. "It won't let us find any tinstones!"
Dad looked up at the dark, grey sky.
"Quick! A storm is on the way. Let's build
our camp!"

# Chapter Three

Dad chopped down branches. Mini stripped the leaves off. Dug sharpened the branch ends with an axe.

Dad marked a circle with a stick.

"Push the branches into the ground,"

he said, as the wind began to blow.

"Now bend the branches over."

The wind blew stronger.

"Weave some more branches around the sides." The wind howled loudly.

"Put the tent skins on top and tie them to the sticks, so the wind can't get in."

The wind made the tent skins flap.

"That's a bad knot!" Dug told Mini.

"It'll come loose."

"I did my best," Mini grumbled.

Dug showed her how to tie a knot.

"You'll need to pull it really tight!"

"You make it look easy!" Mini frowned.

Lightning cracked across the sky!

"Get inside!" said Dad. "Here comes the storm!"

"I'm frightened!" Mini whimpered.

"Here, hold my hand," said Dad.

Thunder and lightning crashed all around them. Dug hugged Woof tightly. The wind shook the tent. One of Mini's bad knots came loose. The wind burst into the tent and lifted it off the ground!

"Hold on to the tent!" Dad yelled.

"Don't let go!"

# Chapter Four

The wind blew hard. The rain lashed in their eyes. Dug held on tight. Woof held on tight. The wind was so strong, it blew them towards the raging river.

"Let go!" Dad yelled. Lightning flashed!
Thunder crashed! Dug didn't hear Dad.
He and Woof held on tight as the tent flew
up into the air!

"Help!" screamed Dug. They crashed into the foaming water.

"Hold on, Woof!" yelled Dug. The wild water swept Dug and woof away.

Then the wind calmed. The rain stopped.

"What if they've drowned?" wailed Mini.

"The river has brought us terrible luck!"

Dad and Mini called out,

"Dug! Woof! Where are you?"

They ran along the riverbank. They
stopped ... and called ... and listened.

"Shhh!" said Dad. "What was that?"

They listened hard.

"Ruff!"

The noise got louder and closer.

"RUFF!"

They ran towards the noise.

# Chapter Five

"There you are!" Dad clapped his hands.

"You're alive!" cheered Mini.

"The tent turned upside down and became

a boat!" laughed Dug. "It brought us to this

island. And look what I've found!"

Dug lifted the biggest tinstone they'd ever
seen high above his head.

"There's lots more where this came from,"
said Dug.

Dad raised his hands in the air.

"Thank you," he called to the river.

"You brought us good luck after all!"

"So, what's my prize for finding the

biggest tinstone?" asked Dug.

"Boiled fish heads for tea!" replied Dad.

"Mmmmm! My favourite!" Dug said,

licking his lips.

# Bronze Age Facts

Copper is a soft metal. If you add a small amount of tin, it turns into bronze. Bronze is a hard metal which can be made into knives, axes and other tools. When tinstones are crushed and melted in a fire, they make small amounts of tin. Tinstones are found in riverbeds or by digging mines underground. Tin was so rare in the Bronze age that merchants came from far away to buy it.

Franklin Watts
First published in Great Britain in 2016 by
The Watts Publishing Group

Text and Illustrations © Shoo Rayner 2016

Series Editor: Melanie Palmer
Series Advisor: Catherine Glavina
Series Designers: Peter Scoulding
and Cathryn Gilbert

ISBN 978 1 4451 4758 1 (hbk)
ISBN 978 1 4451 4760 4 (pbk)
ISBN 978 1 4451 4759 8 (library ebook)

Printed in China

MIX
Paper from
responsible sources
FSC® C104740

Franklin Watts
An imprint of
Hachette Children's Group
Part of The Watts Publishing Group
Carmelite House
50 Victoria Embankment
London EC4Y 0DZ

An Hachette UK Company
www.hachette.co.uk

www.franklinwatts.co.uk